Tiny Troll Treasury
Magic Hair

Written by
Jane Jerrard
Illustrated by
Joe Veno

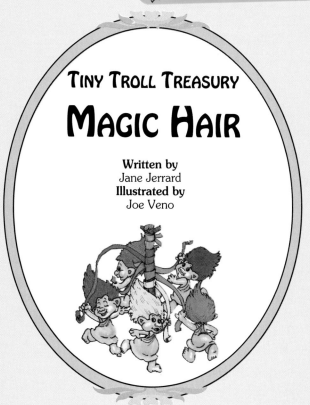

Publications International, Ltd.

A long, long time ago, all trolls looked very much alike. Every troll, young or old, had skin the color of honey and hair the color of oak leaves in autumn.

Trolls were bright-eyed creatures with ready smiles. They loved to have fun and would have been cheerful all the time except for one thing: Each troll found it hard to tell one troll from another troll. They didn't know who was who because everyone looked so much alike.

Imagine how the trolls must have felt. Little Milkweed often followed Buckeye's father home from work. And Chestnut once picked a big bunch of flowers for his girlfriend. But he gave them to Hazelnut's girlfriend by mistake.

Cobweb whispered a secret in the ear of the troll she thought was her best friend. But she whispered in the ear of the very troll who had told her the secret in the first place. And Cobweb had promised not to tell!

Never knowing who was who made the trolls crabby. Their constant bickering disturbed their neighbors, the fairies.

"Those poor trolls," said Rosebud. "Perhaps if we had a party for them they'd forget their troubles and have some fun."

The other fairies, who loved parties, thought this was a wonderful idea. They decided to have the party the very next night.

*E*very troll was invited to the party. At first everyone was excited and happy, but soon the trolls began to worry. How could they go to the fairies' party looking so plain?

The fairies were as colorful and beautiful as butterflies. Each fairy was the color of a flower, and their long hair shimmered in the sunlight. Next to the fairies, the trolls felt dull and drab.

Ivy had a wonderful idea. "We can put berry juice on our hair to make it beautiful colors."

It was worth a try. The trolls gathered berries from the fields and woods. Soon Ladybug's hair was the color of strawberries, Cricket's was as blue as a blueberry, and Oakleaf had grape-colored hair!

On the night of the party, each troll had beautiful berry-colored hair. Best of all, each troll looked different from every other troll.

"We love your pretty hair!" squeaked Iris, speaking for all the fairies.

It was a wonderful party. Everyone danced and little Milkweed rode around the ballroom on her own father's shoulders. Cobweb even knew which troll deserved her apology.

The next day the trolls went down to the stream for their afternoon swim. When they dove into the water, the berry juice washed out of their hair.

As the pretty colors from their hair floated downstream, the trolls began to feel sad. Milkweed asked her father to take her home. "Sorry, little troll," said the big troll, "but I don't think I'm your father."

The trolls were too sad to argue. A hush fell over their village.

In the fairy castle, Rosebud suddenly said, "Do you hear anything?" The other fairies said they didn't. "That's just it! Something must be wrong with the trolls."

The fairies knew what would make the trolls happy. That night while the trolls slept, the fairies touched a magic flower to each troll's hair. The trolls smiled in their sleep, for they dreamed of having colorful hair once again.

The next morning, the fairies heard sounds of joy floating over the hills from the trolls' village. The trolls had awakened to find that their hair was as brightly colored as a flower garden.

The trolls lived happily ever after. Being different was such fun and so exciting!